This
DINOSAUR ROAR!
™

book belongs to

··

For John Smith

Dinosaur Roar! first published in 1994.
This edition first published in 2016 by Macmillan Children's Books
an imprint of Pan Macmillan
20 New Wharf Road, London N1 9RR
Associated companies throughout the world
www.panmacmillan.com

ISBN 978-1-5098-2738-1

10 9 8 7 6 5 4 3 2 1

A CIP catalogue record for this book is available from the British Library.

Printed in China

DINOSAUR ROAR!™

PAUL STICKLAND ❧ HENRIETTA STICKLAND

MACMILLAN CHILDREN'S BOOKS

Dinosaur roar,

dinosaur squeak,

dinosaur fierce,

dinosaur meek,

dinosaur fast,

dinosaur slow,

dinosaur above

and dinosaur below.

Dinosaur weak,

dinosaur strong,

dinosaur short

or very, very long.

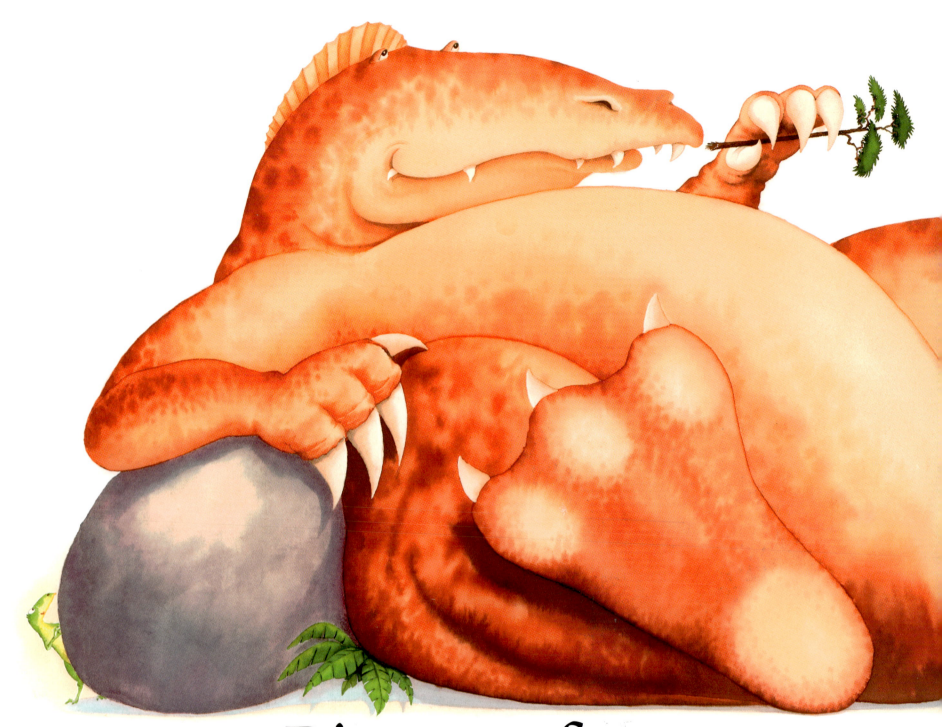

Dinosaur fat,

dinosaur tiny,

dinosaur clean

and dinosaur slimy.

Dinosaur sweet,

dinosaur grumpy,

dinosaur spiky

and dinosaur lumpy.

All sorts of dinosaurs

eating up their lunch,

gobble, gobble, nibble, nibble,

munch, munch, scrunch!

Look out for more

DINOSAUR ROAR!™

titles from Macmillan

Board Book Edition ISBN: 978-1-5098-2808-1

Reviews of Dinosaur Roar!

". . . the picture-book giant for small children . . . one of my favourite books ever to read out loud."

The Times

"The simplicity and comforting rhythms make this instantly appealing."

Independent on Sunday

"This is a delightful book, and a firm favourite with pre-schoolers. The glorious illustrations encourage comment and observation, while the rhythm of the text soon has children chanting along . . ."

Independent

"A lovely rhythmic poem that small children love to recite."

Daily Telegraph

"Based on opposites, the rhyming text has a great swinging rhythm, and the pictures are great too, with some nice visual jokes."

Practical Parenting Magazine

Visit **www.dinosaurroar.com** for more dinosaur fun